Paddle·to·the·Sea

Paddle·to·the·Sea

WRITTEN AND ILLUSTRATED BY

Holling Clancy Holling

Clarion Books
An Imprint of HarperCollins*Publishers*
· Boston New York

ISBN-13: 978-0-395-15082-5
ISBN-10: 0-395-15082-5
ISBN-13: 978-0-395-29203-7/(pbk.)
ISBN-10: 0-395-29203-4/(pbk.)

Manufactured in Vietnam

23 RRDA 55 54 53 52 51 50

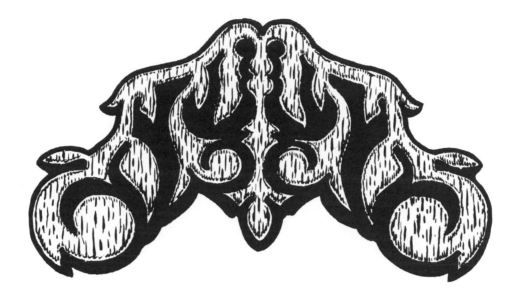

THIS BOOK IS DEDICATED

to

JOHN HENRY CHAPMAN

with whose father I have paddled
under, over, and through many a
Great Lake wave.

Contents

1. HOW PADDLE–TO–THE–SEA CAME TO BE

THE Canadian wilderness was white with snow. From Lake Superior northward the evergreen trees wore hoods and coats of white. A heavy blanket of cloud hung low across the hills. There was no sound. Nothing moved. Even a thread of gray smoke stood up like a pole, keeping the sky from falling on a log cabin in the valley.

Then far off a sound began, grew louder, louder — and swept overhead in a wild cackle of honks and cries. 'Geese!' cried the Indian boy standing in the door of the cabin. 'They come back too soon. I must hurry to finish my Paddle Person!'

He returned to his bear robe by the fire where he had sat for many days whittling a piece of pine. Now he worked on in silence. He bent over the fire to melt lead in an iron spoon, and poured it out to cool and harden in a hollow of the wood. He fastened a piece of tin to one end of the carving. Then he brought out oil paints and worked carefully with a brush.

Satisfied at last, the boy sat back on his heels. Before him lay a canoe one foot long. It looked like his father's big birchbark loaded with packs and supplies for a journey. Underneath was a tin rudder to keep it headed forward, and a lump of lead for ballast. This would keep the canoe low in the water, and turn it right side up after an upset. An Indian figure knelt just back of the middle, grasping a paddle. And along the bottom were carved these words:

2. LONG RIVER REACHING TO THE SEA

NEXT day the Indian boy climbed the hill back of his home. His snowshoes wide as shovels sank into the drifts at every step. When he reached the top he took from his coat the canoe he had made. He then set it in the snow facing southward where, far away, a river cut an icy path through the forest.

'Now I will tell you something!' said the boy to the little figure in the canoe. 'I have learned in school that when this snow in our Nipigon country melts, the water flows to that river. The river flows into the Great Lakes, the biggest lakes in the world. They are set like bowls on a gentle slope. The water from our river flows into the top one, drops into the next, and on to the others. Then it makes a river again, a river that flows to the Big Salt Water.

'I made you, Paddle Person, because I had a dream. A little wooden man smiled at me. He sat in a canoe on a snowbank on this hill. Now the dream has begun to come true. The Sun Spirit will look down at the snow. The snow will melt and the water will run downhill to the river, on down to the Great Lakes, down again and on at last to the sea. You will go with the water and you will have adventures that I would like to have. But I cannot go with you because I have to help my father with the traps.

'The time has come for you to sit on this snowbank and wait for the Sun Spirit to set you free. Then you will be a real Paddle Person, a real Paddle-to-the-Sea.'

THE GREAT LAKES
ARE LIKE BOWLS
ON A HILLSIDE—

3. PADDLE STARTS ON HIS JOURNEY

AT NIGHT wood mice crept over the little canoe. White owls swooped low just to look at it. Rabbits hopped near. Two wolves came to sniff at Paddle; then a wolverine and a weasel.

Each morning when the boy went to make certain that Paddle was safe, he found the tracks in the snow. But he knew that Paddle could not be eaten because he was only painted wood.

All this time the world was changing. The air grew warmer, the birch twigs swelled with new buds. A moose pawed the snow beside a log, uncovering green moss and arbutus like tiny stars. And then, one morning, the gray clouds drifted from the sky. The sun burst out warm and bright above the hills, and under its glare the snow blankets drooped on the fir trees. Everywhere the snow was melting. There was a steady tap-tap-tap of fat drops falling.

The snowbank began to settle under Paddle. Next morning it had split wide open. Across a narrow, deep canyon in the snow, the canoe made a little bridge. But hour by hour it tipped farther forward.

The boy came running over the slippery ground. He was just in time to see the canoe slide down into rushing water. It sank and came to the surface upside down. Then it righted itself and the watching boy saw it plunge forward, leaping on the crest of a brook that dashed downhill.

'Ho!' he called. 'You have started on your journey! Good-by, Paddle-to-the-Sea!'

4. BROOK AND BEAVER POND

THE canoe rushed down a snowy canyon with steep sides. The busy brook backed it, pushed it forward, rolled it under, sent it on, and, finally, dropped it into the quiet water of a pond.

Beavers had made this pond by building a dam of logs and sticks plastered with mud. To do this they had gnawed down trees. The stumps of the trees showed here and there along the banks. In the middle of the pond, the beavers had built their home, an island of sticks with an underwater entrance, safe from enemies. Inside on a shelf above water level, the nest of soft rushes would always be warm and dry.

An old beaver crept out of the water, sleek and dripping, to sit on the roof and scratch himself in the sun. A buck deer waded in the shallows. He had only one antler and the weight of it made him walk with his head turned aside. He swung the antler hard against a stump. It came off easily and dropped into the mud. He shook his head and bounded off into the forest, glad to be free of the weight. By fall he would grow a new set of weapons. A mink dived off a melting snowbank and came up with a fish. A muskrat swam past the drifting canoe and disappeared in the dead rushes. A skunk met a porcupine on a log. Each looked disgusted, turned about, and waddled solemnly away.

The flooding pond burst through a corner of the beaver dam that afternoon. Old leaves, with Paddle in the midst of them, pushed through the gap. Paddle-to-the-Sea was free. The little canoe rushed on with the brook, on toward the river.

5. BREAKUP OF THE RIVER

ON A WARM day, perhaps the very day that the snow had melted and started Paddle on his journey, the breakup of the river had come. All through the winter the river had lain frozen. Wild animals had used it as an ice trail. Lumberjacks had used it as a road for taking their horses and tractors to the logging camps in the forest. But they had not hauled their logs to the sawmill this way. Instead they had piled them up along the frozen banks waiting for the river to carry them when the spring breakup came.

And now it had come. Hundreds of brooks and streams had been flooding the river under its ice. The water, pushing from beneath, forced the ice upward. The banks shook as in an earthquake. Up and down the river the glass pavement cracked all over. The cracks split open. Blocks of ice began to move downstream — faster and faster. A foaming river roared through the forest where the frozen trail had been.

Paddle's canoe tumbled along with the brook until, with one last leap, it shot into the middle of the mad current of the river. The ice and the lumbermen's logs crushed in on every side. Escaping again and again, Paddle raced on. The river rounded a bend. Logs and ice ahead plunged out of sight without warning. Paddle, too, plunged forward, through mist, over the falls.

He was still bottom-side-up in the water when a log rushed over the falls behind him, striking the canoe such a hard blow that it was wedged in a crack of the shaggy bark. And when the log raced away it carried Paddle-to-the-Sea with it, upside down, under water.

6. PADDLE MEETS A SAWMILL

PADDLE's log was four feet thick. Timbers and ice crashed against it, but it floated so low in the water that the canoe, held snugly underneath, was well out of danger. Hours went by, days passed. In time the river widened into a bay dotted with islands, the ice disappeared, and rivermen in spiked boots leaped from log to log prodding them with long pike-poles toward the sawmill.

The mill, a mass of red buildings on stilts above the river bank, opened its wide mouth in the main building. From the mouth ran the log chute, a giant tongue, licking into the water. A heavy chain of spikes moved up the center of the chute, turned over a wheel and returned to the river, an endless belt called a bull-chain. Rivermen pushed the logs onto the spikes which carried them up the chute into the open mouth. A buzzing noise which sometimes became a shriek came from inside the mill. The great saws were at work.

The spikes dug into Paddle's log. The great tree rolled over, bringing Paddle upright and dripping out of the water into the sunlight. The rivermen shouted with surprise as Paddle rode his log up the bull-chain. At the top he was heaved through the door, onto a carrier that looked like a flatcar. Ahead the saw, an endless belt of thin steel, raced so fast its teeth were a blur. Paddle's log was being pushed nearer and nearer to the hungry saw.

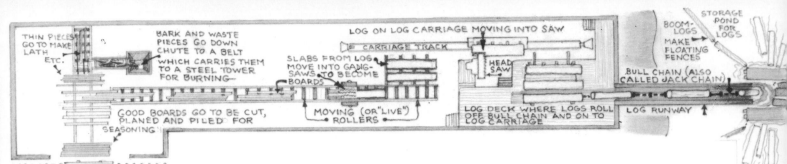

THIN PIECES GO TO MAKE LATH ETC.

BARK AND WASTE PIECES GO DOWN CHUTE TO A BELT WHICH CARRIES THEM TO A STEEL TOWER FOR BURNING

SLABS FROM LOG MOVE INTO GANG-SAWS TO BECOME BOARDS

LOG ON LOG CARRIAGE MOVING INTO SAW

CARRIAGE TRACK

HEAD SAW

STORAGE POND FOR LOGS

BOOM-LOGS MAKE FLOATING FENCES

BULL CHAIN (ALSO CALLED JACK CHAIN)

GOOD BOARDS GO TO BE CUT, PLANED AND PILED FOR SEASONING

MOVING (OR "LIVE") ROLLERS

LOG DECK WHERE LOGS ROLL OFF BULL CHAIN AND ON TO LOG CARRIAGE

LOG RUNWAY

TRAM-CAR ON TRACK FOR MOVING LUMBER

DIAGRAM OF A SAWMILL

7. PADDLE MEETS A FRIEND

THE saw ripped into the end of Paddle's log. The blur of teeth came nearer and nearer. Suddenly a hand snatched Paddle away.

'By Jo!' yelled the lumberjack who had saved him, 'Look what came up the bull-chain! Pretty soon he would be split like a fish. Sit there, my fran. Tonight I take you to my little Henri!' and he laid the carving on a shelf.

The great log moved forward and back, and on each forward trip the band saw ate through it. The wide slabs dropping away slid on rollers to other saws, and came from them as boards. Men pushed the new lumber away on flatcars to unload outside the sawmill. The piles looked like rows of unpainted houses along a street.

After work the lumbermen looked at Paddle. They laughed at the way he had ridden the log into the sawmill. The French-Canadian who had saved him read the message on the bottom of the canoe. Someone wanted the little figure to float to the sea. He would show it to his little boy and then toss it back to the river. But no — Henri would cry if he couldn't keep it. By Jo, best not to tell him at all!

On his way home in the twilight the lumberjack stopped on a bridge. He carved more letters in the canoe. Now the sign read — PLEASE PUT ME BACK IN WATER   I AM PADDLE-TO-THE-SEA FROM NIPIGON COUNTRY, CANADA.

The Frenchman dropped the little canoe off the bridge. 'Have a good voyage!' he said as he watched the river current carry Paddle away into the night.

LAKE NIPIGON →
NIPIGON RIVER →

ISLE ROYAL →

LAKE SUPERIOR is so
big, it could hold Rhode
Island, Connecticut and
3 more states the size
of Massachusetts inside
its outline. It is almost
one quarter mile deep...

8. THE LARGEST LAKE IN THE WORLD

FOR the next few days Paddle, along with old logs, chips, and
bits of boards, drifted on the current of the river. Then the river
widened into a bay with many islands. Paddle floated past them all
until at last there was no land anywhere. Paddle was alone on Lake
Superior, the largest lake in the world.

Only the sky was left — and the sun, and the stars and the water
that slid under him in black valleys or lifted him in blue mountains.
He rode over them in foam before they rolled on and away to the edge
of the sky.

But Paddle was not altogether alone on Lake Superior. One calm
evening his canoe shot upward into the air. It splashed down, only to
be spanked upward again. The glassy eyes of a great fish gazed at him
from below, then disappeared. It had struck at the shiny tin of the
rudder. But Paddle was not food. Another evening a small warbler
swooped down from above and sat on the canoe all night tipping Paddle
half over. Exhausted by its flight across the huge lake the little bird
had found a resting place just in time. At sunrise it flew away on its
journey.

Fish swam under Paddle, gulls soared over him. Ships slid across
the horizon leaving black smoke-trails. Everything was going somewhere, everything except Paddle. He seemed to be sitting in one place
rocking up and down. Yet all the time he had been traveling. Currents
had carried him around the shores of the beaver pond. Now they carried him in Lake Superior in the same way. Paddle, now drifting westward, would someday circle eastward again guided by the shore currents. Steadily and surely they pushed him on — on toward the sea.

THE HILL, THE
BROOK, THE POND →
THE RIVER →
THE SAWMILL →

WHERE
PADDLE
IS NOW

CURRENTS

CURRENTS

9. PADDLE CROSSES TWO BORDERS

ONE night Paddle passed the dim shapes of islands. Morning found him in wide Thunder Bay. Big ships came near churning the water into green froth and tossing Paddle over and over in their waves.

A bumpy line of buildings stretched like castles along the horizon. They were grain elevators at Port Arthur and Fort William filled with mountains of grain which trains had brought from the plains of western Canada. The ships now passing Paddle would carry the grain to other lake ports and other lands, to be made into bread and buns and breakfast foods for millions of people.

A breeze whipped out of the north driving long waves before it. Driftwood followed the waves. A cedar stump came galloping up to Paddle and hooked him between two limbs. Its roots stuck up in the air making a sail which carried Paddle briskly on his way for days until, at last, Paddle and the ferryboat were tossed onto a beach. They had crossed an international border though there was nothing to show for it. They had left Canada and entered the United States. The cedar stump lodged in the sand, shaking Paddle free to ride up and down the beach in foaming surf. Along this beach was a mound of sand which kept the water of a marsh from running into Lake Superior. One long wave heaved Paddle over this barrier and into a lagoon.

Tangled forest formed the marsh's other borders. Lily pads lay on the surface and Paddle's canoe landed on one of them. It was very quiet. The air smelled of mint and wintergreen and pine needles. Paddle had come to rest after two months on restless waves.

10. LIFE IN A NORTHERN MARSH

THE marsh was alive. Dragonflies and butterflies danced in the sun. Turtles lay in rows like buttons on the old logs; and frogs, frightened by stalking herons leaped in all directions. The downy babies of wild ducks pecked eagerly at bugs. Woodpeckers, kingfishers and ruffed grouse made their busy noises. A cow moose with her calf splashed in the lagoon to drive off flies.

Near Paddle, a bull moose, now growing new antlers, was feeding on the roots and stems of water lilies. With his head far under water, he jerked the lily pad from under Paddle's canoe and set him free to be pushed about on the pond by the wind.

Days passed. When it was sunny squirrels chattered in the pines and chipmunks scolded from high rocks. But they were silent and the ducks moved to safety on the day that a mother bear and her twins came to romp in the water. The cubs caught crayfish and frogs in the mud, while the mother bear squatted on a rock beside a deep pool in the lagoon and smacked a black bass to the bank with her paw. After this picnic all three ripped open rotted stumps for grubs and beetles.

Paddle might have been caught in the marsh for life. But one evening no stars came out. Thunder crashed and lightning split the night with fire. A wet owl flapped madly for shelter in the forest; ducks squawked and gathered their babies under mossy banks; a water-soaked muskrat waddled wetly into a hollow log and sat down with a very sour look.

The rain made a thick curtain. The pond rose inch by inch. Part of the sandy mound along the brook gave way. Torn lily plants, loose wood and islands of watercress raced out to Lake Superior. Paddle was again on his way to the sea.

11. PADDLE FINDS ONE END OF LAKE SUPERIOR

PADDLE traveled steadily westward along the north shore of Lake Superior. Sometimes lake currents pushed him forward a mile every hour. At other times, when breezes pulled him backward off his course, he took five hours to travel a mile.

This was a wilderness shore, but Paddle was never alone. He had for company the gulls who nested on the rocky islands and flew up like clouds of smoke from the rocks. Indians paddled canoes among the bays, and fishermen lived along the shore in shacks and spread out their nets to dry. Sometimes towns, like toy blocks, broke the line of dark pines that was the mainland; or rivers, running from hidden lakes in the forest, cut through the cliffs in waterfalls like giant stairs of silver. At night loons called mournfully from the water and wolves howled back from the land.

Two months after leaving the marsh Paddle reached the western and very narrow end of Lake Superior, where bridges crossed from shore to shore. He had come to Duluth, Minnesota, a city on a hill. Later he drifted over a wide river to Superior, Wisconsin, on a flat plain. At these ports many ships were loading barrels of butter, crates of eggs and boxes of vegetables. Others were piled high with lumber for distant cities. But most of the ships at the docks were unloading coal from Indiana and Ohio and reloading iron ore. Paddle bumped against the piling of a long dock. High above him, a train was dumping the ore down pipes into a ship's hold. The train had brought this ore, that stained everything red, from the largest iron mine in the world for which this region is famous.

Paddle floated beneath one of the docks in brick-red water. Red dust sifted down on him.

Loon

Freighter —
loading iron ore
at an ore dock

ONTARIO, CANADA

DULUTH

PADDLE
IS NOW
HERE

SUPERIOR

MINNESOTA | WISCONSIN | MICHIGAN

12. A FISH STORY

'BEST catch in weeks!' one man was saying. 'And that's not all — look! we're even netting red Injuns in canoes!'

Paddle, stained red with iron ore had traveled eastward from Superior for a week. Now he had reached the Apostle Islands, one of the best fishing regions of Lake Superior, and had been caught in one of the fishermen's nets. Wooden floats held the upper edges of these nets on the surface. Lead weights pulled the lower edges downward like a fence in the water. Two men in a motorboat had hauled him in. Large fish, three times larger than his canoe, flopped about him. There were so many that they filled big boxes and overflowed into the boat until the men worked knee-deep in lake trout and whitefish.

The men paused only for a moment to look at Paddle. When all the net was aboard, the boat sped for an island and tied up at a wobbly dock. Three more men and their wives, five dogs and two cats came down to help. The fish were cleaned on the dock — a messy business, but the dogs and cats liked it, and the greedy gulls who ate the refuse thrown into the water. Everyone hurried to get the fresh fish packed in cracked ice and stored in a shed.

When the last fish was packed away, one of the fishermen looked around. 'Where's that other fish we caught?' he asked. 'That Injun in a canoe?' But Paddle could not be found. In the excitement he had slipped through a hole in the dock and into the water.

The men took the nets from the boat and stretched them on big reels to dry and to be mended. They loaded fresh nets aboard and then roared away to set them for a new catch. A large boat came to take the fish stored in the shed to the mainland for shipment to far-away markets. Paddle was forgotten.

PADDLE

APOSTLE
ISLANDS

HOLLING

BARS OF
KEEWEENAW COPPER
READY FOR SHIPPING

13. ADRIFT AGAIN

STORMS swept over the lake, making great waves that washed Paddle out of his prison under the dock. Storms followed him nearly all the three hundred miles that he traveled during the next month, crossing and recrossing his watery trails. One wild afternoon a yellow spear of lightning struck a tree on a cliff, splitting it from top to bottom.

The boy who made Paddle could have told him that the old Indians believed the lightning flashed when a Thunderbird struck its prey, and that thunder rolled from the beat of its mighty wings. But the boy had been to school and he could have told Paddle how rivers are made to turn dynamos; and how powerful electric currents come from the dynamos and follow copper cables to light homes and run factories and radios. But the boy was far away now and Paddle was following a long river to the sea.

When no wind blew, the currents carried him eastward on his way. For a while he saw no land because he was riding the main shipping lanes of Lake Superior. Big freighters passed him and he played his old game of loop-the-loop in their wakes. He passed the Keweenaw Peninsula, the country of copper mines. Indians, long ago, had mined this copper to make knives and arrowheads, trading it as far away as Mexico. Now-a-days, copper is made into such things as pennies, cooking pots, and electric cables.

After passing the Keweenaw Peninsula, Paddle was often washed ashore; and each time, storms tossed him back into the lake. In between storms, wolves howled and hunted under a cold, white moon. Foxes searched the beach for a wave-tossed fish. Buck deer with new antlers and does without them came down to the shore. Ducks flocked in the marshes. It was Fall.

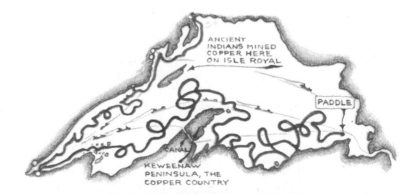

ANCIENT
INDIANS MINED
COPPER HERE
ON ISLE ROYAL

PADDLE

CANAL

KEWEENAW
PENINSULA, THE
COPPER COUNTRY

14. THE SHIPWRECK

ONE day Paddle was smothered on foaming crests and lost in deep valleys. The late fall storms for which Lake Superior is famous had overtaken him. Waves rushed with bristling manes like packs of wolves. Strong gales lashed them into bigger and bigger waves until they were higher than a house. When spray struck Paddle, it froze instantly.

Near Paddle a freighter crept out of the storm. Ice, the terror of captains and crews on the late fall runs, had made her a shapeless mass. The ship wallowed and rolled and seemed to be out of control.

Then in the darkness ahead a star flickered and flashed. A lighthouse was signaling that help was at hand. The ship seemed to find new power as the doomed men fought toward hope of land. A lifeboat appeared, rowing slowly toward the ship like a water beetle swimming toward a whale. A coiled line shot in spirals across the icy deck, was caught, and a stout cable was hauled aboard. Then the lifeboat rowed off with the other end of the cable. The ship reared up and crashed down heavily, tossing Paddle high in the air. Men ran forward along the deck, just as the freighter broke in two. The boilers blew up, the stern half sank in foam and explosions, but the bow end lay on jagged rocks with men clinging to it like tired flies.

Paddle, rushed forward by the surf, skidded up the beach near the lighthouse and a Coast Guard Station. A lifeline that had been attached to the wrecked ship stretched to the shore. And dangling from it by a pulley above the reaching surf, a man was being hauled in by a breeches buoy. Trip by trip the men of the lost ship were saved. Paddle, on the beach, was saved too. He had escaped Lake Superior's icy water and violent storms.

DAVY JONES'S LOCKER

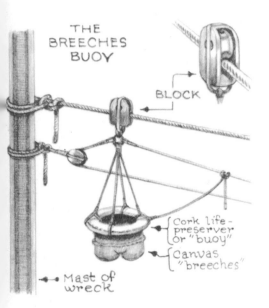

THE
BREECHES
BUOY

BLOCK

Cork life-
preserver
or "buoy"

Canvas
"breeches"

Mast of
wreck

15. DRY DOCK

'YES, I know that if one sunken ship were placed every half mile, the line of wrecks would reach from end to end of the Great Lakes chain. But that doesn't make *me* feel any better, now that *my* ship has joined them in Davy Jones's Locker!' The captain of the wrecked freighter had been talking to the crew of the Coast Guard Station while his men were getting into warm, dry clothes.

The rescued men were soon driven off in trucks and the Coast Guard crew took time to look at Paddle. He had been found after the wreck and set on a table among charts and brass instruments.

The men knew from Paddle's carved sign that he had started his travels near Nipigon. They guessed from his red ore stains that he went somewhere near Duluth. He must have gone, they figured on a chart, about seven hundred miles.

'You haven't allowed for winds blowing him all over the map,' said one of them called Bill. 'Two thousand miles would be more like it. He sure needs repairs. Paddle has traveled some, but he hasn't reached the sea yet. It's dry dock for him right now, or he never will.'

So that is how Paddle got a new copper rudder that would not rust; new paint (with the canoe bright red); and a waterproof coating of ship's varnish. And, best of all, a thick copper plate replaced the lead ballast. Bill stamped small letters deep into this plate. Now the sign read:

'I am Paddle-to-the-Sea, from Nipigon Country north of Lake Superior. This plate, containing original message with more added, was put on at Whitefish Bay after a shipwreck. Please help me to more adventures. Scratch with metal point on this copper, names of towns I pass. Return me to water in good place to continue voyage to sea.'

ICE-BOUND
AT THE SOO

16. BY DOG SLED TO THE SOO

PADDLE stayed at the Coast Guard Station until Winter, and then Bill carried out a plan he had made. He telephoned a friend at 'The Soo.'

This is what people call Sault Ste. Marie, twin cities that lie one in Canada, one in Michigan, with St. Mary's River as a boundary between. Ships cannot pass down the roaring rapids at this point. Instead they go around the rapids by means of locks built like huge stairs, then follow St. Mary's River to Lake Huron. When the river freezes, the ships tie up at The Soo to await the Spring breakup.

When Bill's friend, the Mate on an ice-bound freighter, answered the telephone, the Coast Guard crew gathered around to listen.

'Hello, Maloney? This is Bill. Say, after that last wreck we picked up an Indian in a canoe. Yeah. Came two thousand miles from Nipigon,' and Bill swung the receiver so his pals could listen.

'JUM-ping WHITE-fish!' boomed a voice. 'HOW did he EVER ——'

'Yeah,' Bill continued, 'and he doesn't speak English. Now, sometime you'll be running to Buffalo. You're to take him and his canoe with you ——'

'*HEY!*' The yell could be heard across the room. 'My freighter doesn't take passengers! *INDian — caNOE — ARE YOU CRAZY?*'

'I'm sending him with Pierre, the trapper you're acquainted with. GOOD–BY!' and Bill slammed down the receiver. 'I guess that will worry him some,' he chuckled, and everyone else roared.

A few days later Pierre tucked Paddle under his bundle of furs, and was off for a sixty mile run by dog sled to The Soo.

THE WRECK

WHITEFISH
BAY

SAULT
STE.
MARIE

PADDLE'S
TRIP TO
THE SOO

SAULT
STE.
MARIE

ONTARIO

MICHIGAN

LAKE HURON

HOLLING

① SHIP COMES INTO LOCK

DIRECTION OF CURRENT

② REAR GATES CLOSE — WATER IN LOCK SINKS AS VALVES UNDER FRONT GATES OPEN

③ FRONT GATES OPEN

④ SHIP STEAMS OUT OF LOCK, LEAVING IT READY FOR ANOTHER SHIP HEADED UP-STREAM.

AMERICAN LOCKS AT THE SOO

CANADIAN LOCKS ARE ACROSS ST. MARY'S RIVER AND RAPIDS

17. NON–STOP DOWN LAKE MICHIGAN

AT THE SOO, Pierre soon found Maloney's ore boat. The Mate was writing out a report when the trapper stepped into his cabin.

'*YOU?*' exploded Maloney. 'GET OUT! AND TAKE THAT INDIAN WITH YOU!'

'You take him, and his canoe,' drawled Pierre, setting Paddle on the desk.

'What? Where?' gasped the Mate.

At dinner he heard the whole story. 'Well, you can tell Bill that Paddle goes to Buffalo with me, safe and sound!' he laughed.

When Spring came, Maloney's ship moved into a huge concrete chamber with solid steel gates at both ends. Valves at the bottom let the water out slowly, and the big boat sank with the water level. Then the last gate opened, and Paddle was on his way down the St. Mary's River. But not, this trip, to Buffalo. Two days later Paddle had reached Gary, a city of steel mills at the south end of Lake Michigan.

Here Mate Maloney scratched 'Gary, Indiana' after 'The Soo' on Paddle's copper plate and bundled him into a canvas seaman's bag with his soiled clothes. After unloading its iron ore, his ship was to go to drydock for repairs, and he had to move to another of the steel company's boats.

While carrying the Mate's luggage, a clumsy deck hand dropped the bag overboard, and waves washed it out of reach. Mate Maloney made the air blue with words. How could he ever face Bill again? But it was no use; his ship was waiting.

So Paddle was left behind, all tied up with shirts and socks in a sack. But worse, he was at the South end of Lake Michigan, off his direct route to the sea.

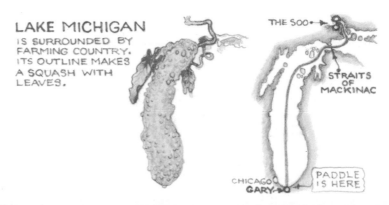

LAKE MICHIGAN IS SURROUNDED BY FARMING COUNTRY. ITS OUTLINE MAKES A SQUASH WITH LEAVES.

THE SOO

STRAITS OF MACKINAC

CHICAGO
GARY

PADDLE IS HERE

18. PADDLE RETURNS TO THE NORTH

A WEEK after leaving the boat at Gary, the well-soaked bag drifted ashore. Playful dogs tore it apart. A puppy carried Paddle up and down the beach, dropping him, at last, to bark at a wave.

Paddle was free again to explore the long beach that formed the southern end of Lake Michigan. Sand dunes rolled eastward along this Indiana coast. Spring bathers covered the shores. Paddle escaped them all, though he was buried and uncovered many times by the waves.

The lake shore curved, and lazy currents carried Paddle northward. The endless beach was littered with cast-away things. Paddle was often tossed among heaps of pebbles, shells, fish bones, bottles and barrels. All about were boxes, broken oars, timbers with twisted spikes and rusty chains, and sometimes the wreck of a ship that once had sailed.

Summer found him halfway up the Michigan coast. He passed green meadows where cows stood in the brooks and horses kept to the shade. Hot breezes rippled the grain and windmills sang out of tune. Wagonloads of hay creaked into fat barns. Summer faded and autumn came. Vines were heavy with grapes, and orchards were loaded with apples. Corn shocks made Indian teepees over the hills, and the coast glowed yellow and scarlet with fall colors.

The fields gave way to pine forests. Nights were filled with the lonely cry of the loon. Paddle had traveled south through Lake Michigan in two days. It had taken him three seasons to return to the northern end of the lake, on his way to the sea.

19. FOREST FIRE

ONE cold Fall morning Paddle stranded on a tiny island of rock. A quarter of a mile away lay a rounded bay with a beach bordered by forest. The morning was peaceful, but toward late afternoon a cloud of smoke hung over the wilderness. Ashes fell into the water like snow, then hot sparks, until at last a forest fire raged across the wooded hills.

The flames came nearer and nearer. They reached the lake shore a mile each side of the bay, cutting off escape by land. Three rabbits hopped out of the brush and squatted on the beach. They did not move when a lynx trotted past. Two does crashed out of the timber. A fox and a martin rushed frantically over the driftwood. Mad with fear, these animals paid no attention to each other. Their numbers increased and all of them, from bears to mice, tried to reach Paddle's island. Some of these creatures managed to survive the waves and crawled out near the little canoe. They gasped for breath, and held their noses near the surface of the water where the air was not so thick with smoke.

The fire roared like a hurricane all night. It swept to the bay until the shores became a wall of heat and flame. The whole world seemed to be on fire.

All next day the terrified animals clung to the rock island or swam in aimless circles in the ash-filled water. Gradually the fire died down. A few black poles and hills bare of everything but ashes were all that remained of the forest. One by one the animals swam to the beach to travel for miles in search of a new forest home. The waves freed Paddle again and he, too, left his island refuge and the blackened shores.

20. THROUGH LAKE HURON

WHILE Paddle was drifting through the Straits of Mackinac into Lake Huron, Winter came. The water changed to ice, freezing Paddle to the shore. But men and boys from near-by towns, who fished in shanties over holes cut in the ice, accidentally freed him with their sleds. Pushed by howling winds, Paddle skated on his copper plate for hundreds of miles over Lake Huron.

Lake Huron knew all about canoes, though it had probably never seen one skate before. The Indian tribes that had once lived in this territory had built some of the best birchbark canoes in America. The French had copied the Indians, finding canoes light and easy to carry around beaver dams and river rapids or for portaging from lake to lake when there were no streams. Even today the canoe is still the best craft for traveling the water-trails of the forests.

Spring came and Paddle was two years old. His paint, protected by Bill's waterproof varnish, was in good condition, and a winter's skating had polished his copper plate like new. The ice cracked into cakes, drifted southward, and carried Paddle along.

A young girl on her father's motorboat picked Paddle out of the water of Saginaw Bay one day in early summer. She read his message and scratched 'Bay City, Michigan' after 'Gary, Indiana.' Then she planned a great launching, but her father read 'Return me to water in good place to continue voyage to sea' and decided that the currents were too slow in Lake St. Clair.

So Paddle, sitting comfortably on a little girl's lap, completed his crossing of Lake Huron, and was on his way to Detroit.

LAKE HURON, in the country of the old French and Indian trappers, makes the outline of a trapper with a pack of furs.

Red iron ore, the life blood of INDUSTRY, flows into a HEART and out through a great TRADE ARTERY, to supply the nation with steel.

LAKE HURON

PORT HURON SARNIA

ST. CLAIR RIVER

DETROIT

LAKE ST. CLAIR

WINDSOR

DETROIT RIVER

MICH. ONTARIO

PADDLE COMES TO LAKE ERIE

TOLEDO

OHIO

21. PADDLE REACHES LAKE ERIE

As THE motorboat chugged lazily down the St. Clair River, with Michigan on one bank facing Canada on the other, it passed farms and summer cottages and came to marshy little Lake St. Clair. Here the water was so shallow that buoys with lights and clanging bells had to mark out a course for ships. After crossing this lake, the boat entered a wide river and stopped at Detroit, and here Paddle's plate received another name.

The girl's father, who worked at one of the Detroit factories, took Paddle to his office. When one of his friends who had a museum filled with curiosities of the Great Lakes offered to buy him, the girls' father shook his head.

'No,' he said, 'somewhere, someone who had faith in currents, in winds — and also in people, put thought and careful work into this carving. And I'll not be the one to stop his Paddle-to-the-Sea.'

Paddle stayed a week in Detroit. Ore boats unloaded their red ore beside the factory that would turn it into thousands of bright new automobiles. At the end of his week Paddle again went in the motorboat with the girl and her father, this time down the Detroit River. Ferryboats running between the United States and Canada chugged across their bow. Canoes with picnickers, rowboats with silent fishermen, passenger steamers noisy with dance music, passed by. Big buildings dropped astern. Green fields replaced them, and a Coast Guard Station, trim and white, and islands with lighthouses. Then the shore dropped away and the motorboat stopped. There was a splash.

'Here's Lake Erie, Paddle-to-the-Sea,' cried the girl. 'Good-by and good luck.'

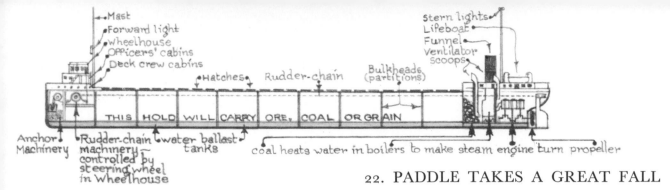

Mast
Forward light
Wheelhouse
Officers' cabins
Deck crew cabins
Hatches.
Rudder-chain
Bulkheads (partitions)
stern lights
Lifeboat
Funnel
Ventilator scoops

THIS HOLD WILL CARRY ORE, COAL OR GRAIN

Anchor Machinery
Rudder-chain machinery — controlled by steering wheel in Wheelhouse
water ballast tanks
coal heats water in boilers to make steam engine turn propeller

DIAGRAM OF A LAKE FREIGHTER

22. PADDLE TAKES A GREAT FALL

IN THE cities along the coast of Lake Erie, Paddle traveled in smoke and steam — dust and heat — naked flame and the clanging noises of commerce. There were tall black towers against red flashes of fire. Tons of white-hot metal lighting the insides of steel mills. Mountains of black coal, ridges of red ore. And, controlling it all, men who seemed to run around without reason, less important than ants. Ships were everywhere — loaded, empty, silent at the docks; ships in the harbor drawn by fussy fat tugs; in the rivers hooting for drawbridges to let them through.

By the time Paddle reached Buffalo, New York, he had added to his plate 'Toledo,' 'Sandusky,' 'Cleveland,' 'Ashtabula' in Ohio; 'Erie' in Pennsylvania; and 'Port Colborne' in Canada. Steel-workers, mechanics, engineers, sailors, all kept him a while and sent him on. His photograph got into the newspapers and went north with the boats. Bill, at Whitefish Bay saw the picture and sighed with satisfaction. Mate Maloney saw it and sighed with relief. The girl's father framed it for his office.

Paddle missed the paper excitement for some real excitement of his own. Ships take the Welland Canal around Niagara Falls. Paddle didn't.

'Mother! LOOK! A little MAN! In a BOAT!' a child screamed. She stood with the usual crowd of people gathered this bright summer day in the beautiful Canadian park overlooking the falls. Everyone jumped and came running, just in time to see Paddle plunge over the green edge and drop down . . . down . . . down. . . .

LAKE ERIE lies in a land of coal mines and steel mills. Its outline makes a lump of coal.

ONTARIO
WELLAND CANAL
NIAGARA FALLS
PORT COLBORNE
BUFFALO
PADDLE'S TRIP THROUGH LAKE ERIE
NEW YORK
MICH.
ERIE
TOLEDO
ASHTABULA
SANDUSKY
CLEVELAND
OHIO
PENNSYLVANIA

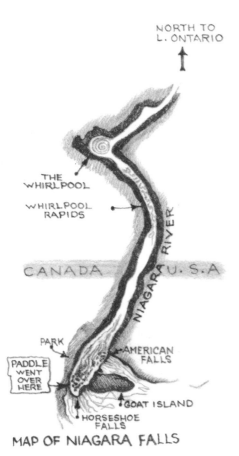

GOAT ISLAND

← PADDLE WENT OVER THIS EDGE OF
HORSESHOE FALLS ON THE
CANADIAN SIDE —
160 FEET HIGH AND 2600 FEET WIDE

NIAGARA FALLS ON THE
AMERICAN SIDE IS
JUST ABOVE —
165 FEET HIGH AND
1000 FEET WIDE

NORTH TO
L. ONTARIO

THE
WHIRLPOOL

WHIRLPOOL
RAPIDS

NIAGARA RIVER

CANADA U.S.A

PARK

AMERICAN
FALLS

PADDLE
WENT
OVER
HERE

GOAT ISLAND

HORSESHOE
FALLS

MAP OF NIAGARA FALLS

LAKE ONTARIO
lies in farming country.
Its outline makes
a carrot.

THE THOUSAND
ISLANDS
KINGSTON

TORONTO

ST. LAWRENCE
RIVER

23. LAKE ONTARIO — AT LAST

THE lower half of the Falls was hidden in mist with a rainbow across it. Paddle fell through the rainbow and went on falling. There was a swirling, boiling, hissing, churning, and then Paddle went under.

Paddle had ridden rapids. There had been his first brook, back in the forest, wild enough for its size. Then he had ridden the mad river, and seen the rapids at The Soo, so fierce that ships went around them. But *these* rapids! Thirty-foot waves rushed like shooting stars, turning inside-out at every jump. Paddle flew up on a chain of wet volcanoes, plunged deep in submarine dives, and took sudden trips toward the moon in green rockets.

Far from the falls he came to the surface, rolled over and over down the Niagara River and into a whirlpool, where it seemed that all the water in the Great Lakes suddenly decided to run back uphill. Paddle bumped into huge timbers and trees that had whirled at a giddy pace for years, unable to escape. By some miracle he got past this never-stop-merry-go-round after a day — or maybe a week.

And then, at last, Paddle floated into the calm water of Lake Ontario. Black coots and white terns looked him over. Kindly people picked him up. Someone took him to Toronto, someone else to Kingston and through the Thousand Islands. The dizzy fall lay behind, the sea ahead.

24. ALONG THE GREAT RIVER

PADDLE spent that winter in Canada with a little old lady who lived beside the St. Lawrence River near Montreal. Paddle joined her collection of Indian, French and British curios of early Canada. An American boy visiting in Montreal liked to listen to her stories of the St. Lawrence. She called it 'the River.'

'The Indian name for the River was Canada,' she said one day. 'Yes, the French took that name for this country and called the River "St. Lawrence." Nowadays, with canals dug around its rapids, some of the biggest ships come a thousand miles from the sea to Montreal. This is a skyscraper city today, but it started as a trading post.

'And Quebec was a trading post, too. See that piece of birchbark sewn with split roots? Two hundred years ago it was part of a Huron Indian canoe that rode the River. Every Spring Indian canoes with many paddlers brought beaver pelts to the French at these posts.

'Yes, Frenchmen explored the River and the Lakes. Champlain, called the "Father of New France," was the first governor of Canada at Quebec. He discovered the Lakes, and fought the Iroquois. The Hurons loved him, but the Iroquois hated all Frenchmen and, in the end, helped the English to get Canada. But whole towns along the River still speak French to this day, and Montreal is the third largest French-speaking city in the world.

'Yes,' she said, peering over her spectacles, 'the River has made history. Wish I knew it all. Paddle, here, comes from where the River really starts, in the hills above Lake Superior. Long journey. Come Spring, I'll give him back to the River and send him along to the sea.'

FORT MACKINAC

SAULT STE. MARIE

LAKE NIPISSING

FRENCH R.

THIS IS THE OLD ROUTE OF THE FUR CANOES TO MONTREAL

OTTAWA RIVER

DIONNE QUINTUPLETS BORN HERE

HURON COUNTRY AND THE LAKE OF THE HURONS

OTTAWA present capital of Canada

THE ST. LAWRENCE RIVER

QUEBEC Champlain's capital OF NEW FRANCE

MONTREAL — the end of the fur trail from the UPPER LAKES —

LAKE CHAMPLAIN where Champlain fought the Iroquois

TO FORT DETROIT

LAKE ONTARIO

IROQUOIS COUNTRY

NEWFOUNDLAND

GULF OF ST. LAWRENCE

PADDLE comes to the GRAND BANKS.

QUEBEC

MONTREAL

ST. LAWRENCE R.

L. ONTARIO

PORTLAND

L. ERIE

BOSTON

NEW YORK

WASHINGTON

25. RIVERS IN THE SEA

Spring came again, with new leaves like crumpled lace in the maples, and Paddle was three years old. True to her promise, the old lady took Paddle to the River and set him free again.

A few weeks later Paddle passed the high bluffs of Quebec. Then came mountains, the river widened, and forests lined the shores. Strange fish swam by in water that was now salty. French fishermen caught long eels by thousands. But Paddle had not yet reached the sea. The river, now wide as Lake Michigan, ran into the Gulf of St. Lawrence. Now he encountered tides. He was stranded on a rock for six hours while the water slipped away. Then for another six hours the water rushed back, swept him off his perch and raced him miles upstream. He had been caught in the battle of river current and sea tide — a battle that had been going on endlessly since the world began.

After this, Paddle was out of sight of land for months. He caught the Gulf Stream, a warm wide river in the sea running from the Gulf of Mexico along the American coast and northeast toward Europe. Then he ran into fog and the gray shadow of land. This was Newfoundland, and here Paddle met another river in the sea, the icy Labrador Current that sweeps down from the Arctic, hits the tropic stream and causes fogs.

Paddle passed fishing boats and countless fish brought to the famous Grand Banks of Newfoundland by the Labrador Current. Paddle had reached the most famous fishing ground in the world. And he had reached the Sea!

RIVERS IN THE SEA

LABRADOR CURRENT

CANADA

GREAT LAKES

NEWFOUND-LAND

EUROPE

U.S.A.

GULF STREAM

GULF OF MEXICO

AFRICA

SO. AMERICA

26. PADDLE FINDS A NEW FRIEND

SOMEWHERE off the Grand Banks, a French boat with full cargo of fish was under sail for home. The Captain noticed an odd little something near the bow. A boy ran down the deck crying, 'I'll get it, Papa.' He waved an old dip-net lashed to a pole. And so, in the foggy gray dawn, up came Paddle-to-the-Sea.

The boy's father was a man who knew many things. And as he cleaned the copper plate under the canoe, he was filled with wonder, for he could read Paddle's trail. With his son beside him, he traced the long journey on a chart.* He could only guess at part of it, and could not know it all.

The boy looked at Paddle lashed by fish line above his bunk. Wave and wind had worn him smooth and there was little of his second coat of paint left. But he still smiled, and the boy liked his smile. It made Paddle look as though he had seen many things and understood them all.

'A long journey, you have made,' the boy would say. 'Now you are on a ship. Do you hear the wind in the rigging? Do you feel the roll of the waves? Do you know that you are sailing across a great ocean to France? Are you not surprised?'

But Paddle never showed surprise. For four years he had been what he was supposed to be, a Paddle-to-the-Sea. And he had done what he was supposed to do. And so he showed no surprise, even at crossing the ocean.

* There is a map at end of book.

27. ON A WHARF

IT WAS Spring in Nipigon Country, north of Lake Superior. Along the swirling river the air was sweet with the smell of pine and green, growing things.

Three men stood on a wharf at a town, near a sawmill.

'Why doesn't that good-for-nothing guide get here!' said one, fussing with his fishing tackle. 'I've made a long journey from the City, to catch trout!'

'Oh, that guide — he come sometime,' said the second, a French-Canadian lumberjack. He went on cutting the strings from a bundle of newspapers. 'But you talk 'bout long journey. You see these paper? Jus' now in the mail she come from my cousin, in France! By Jo, *that* is one *real* long journey, no?' and he lit his pipe, unrolling the papers on an overturned box.

'Us Frenchmans, we get lonesome for mail that speaks French,' he continued with a sigh. Suddenly he stopped short. 'By Jo!' he gasped. 'You see *that?* Looka that picture!'

'What's the matter?' said the other, looking up. 'Huh. Photograph of a toy. Little Indian in a canoe. Yeah, he's cute.'

'Cute? It is wonderful! Look quick. The paper, she say — this little man floats from Nipigon Country — down Great Lakes to St. Lawrence Gulf — French fish-boat, she pick him out of Ocean an' take him to my cousin's town! An' by Jo! You know what?' — and the lumberjack was dancing up and down, waving the paper — '*I* am the one who saved him from the saws! By all the Saints, I did it! *Me!* Years back I put him in the river! Oh! I mus' tell my Henri! By Jo, *you* talk 'bout long journey!'

The third man on the wharf was a young Indian, tall and strong. In his moccasins he moved so silently across the dock that the others did not hear him. He took one long look over the Frenchman's shoulder at the paper.

'You put him back in the river and sent him on? Good. I made that one,' he said softly, and turned away.

The young man had stepped into his canoe before the Frenchman spoke again. 'What that Injun say jus' now?' he asked, laying the paper aside.

'Didn't hear him,' replied the sportsman. Both of them glanced toward the river, but the canoe was already moving away under steady strokes of the paddle. So the two men returned to their own important thoughts.

In the canoe, the Indian smiled. Once he paused in a stroke, and rested his blade. For that instant he looked like his own Paddle. There was a song in his heart. It crept to his lips, but only the water and the wind could hear.

'You, Little Traveler! You made the journey, the Long Journey. You now know the things I have yet to know. You, Little Traveler! You were given a name, a true name in my father's lodge. Good Medicine, Little Traveler! You are truly a Paddle Person, a Paddle-to-the-Sea!'

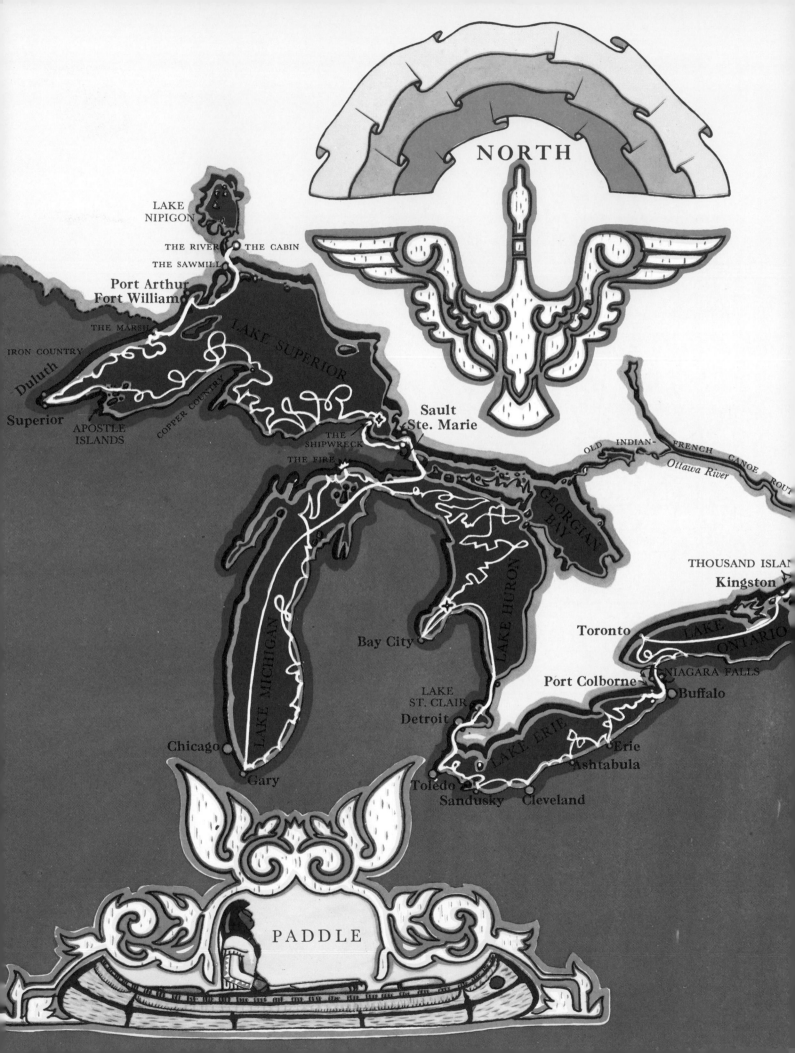

NORTH

LAKE NIPIGON

THE RIVER   THE CABIN
THE SAWMILL
Port Arthur
Fort William
THE MARSH
IRON COUNTRY
Duluth
Superior
APOSTLE ISLANDS
COPPER COUNTRY
LAKE SUPERIOR
THE SHIPWRECK
THE FIRE
Sault Ste. Marie

GEORGIAN BAY

OLD INDIAN—FRENCH CANOE ROUTE
Ottawa River

THOUSAND ISLAND
Kingston

LAKE MICHIGAN

LAKE HURON

Bay City

Toronto

LAKE ONTARIO

Port Colborne
NIAGARA FALLS
Buffalo

LAKE ST. CLAIR
Detroit

Chicago

Gary

Toledo
Sandusky
LAKE ERIE
Cleveland
Ashtabula
Erie

PADDLE

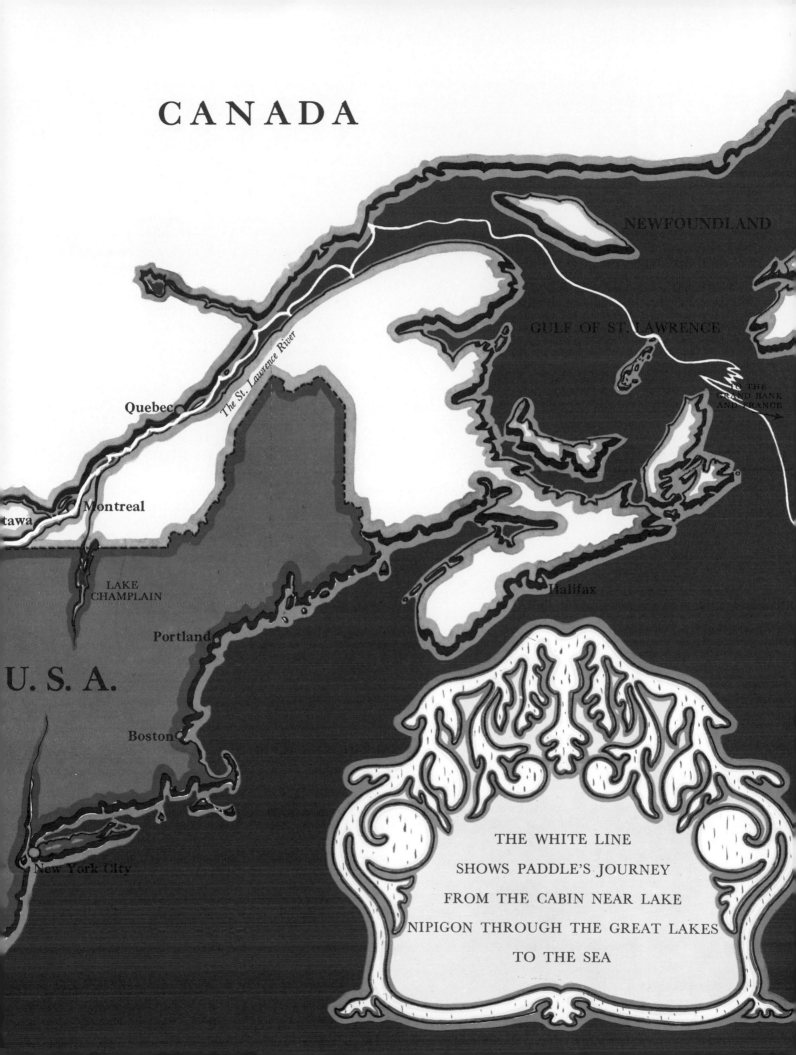